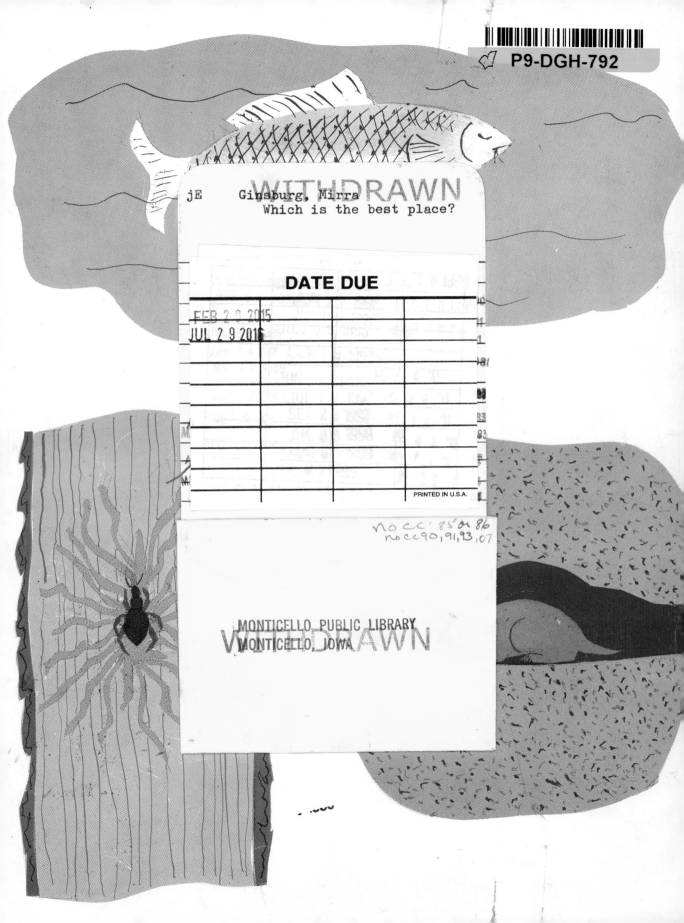

jE Ginsburg, Mirra
WITHDRAWN
Which is the best place?

DATE DUE

FEB 2 9 2015
JUL 2 9 2016

PRINTED IN U.S.A.

noccc '85 or 86
nocc 90, 91, 93, 07

Which Is the
Best Place?

Which Is the Best Place?

Adapted from the Russian of Pyotr Dudochkin by
MIRRA GINSBURG
Pictures by
ROGER DUVOISIN

Macmillan Publishing Co., Inc.
NEW YORK
Collier Macmillan Publishers
LONDON

Macmillan Publishing Co., Inc., 866 Third Avenue, New York, N.Y. 10022
Collier Macmillan Canada, Ltd.
Printed in the United States of America
1 2 3 4 5 6 7 8 9 10

Library of Congress Cataloging in Publication Data
Ginsburg, Mirra. Which is the best place?
SUMMARY: The rooster on the fence and the goose
on the grass argue about which place is best and get
a different answer from each animal friend they consult.
[1. Animals—Fiction] I. Dudochkin, Petr Petrovich.
Gde luchshe. II. Duvoisin, Roger Antoine, date
III. Title.   PZ7.G43896Wh   [E]
75-31946   ISBN 0-02-735980-8

To Paul

A goose met a rooster in the village street.
"Ga-ga-ga!" gabbled the goose. "How are you today?"
"Cock-a-doodle-doo!" sang the rooster. "I'm fine.
  I've been gathering seed all morning."

He flew up and perched on the fence
in the shade of a tree.
There he sat, flapping his wings and crowing.

"And I've been nibbling grass all morning,"
  said the goose.
  She chose a place by the fence, on the fresh
  green grass, pulled up one leg, hid her head
  under her wing, and rested, standing on one foot.

"Hey, goose," said the rooster, "come up here
  and sit on the perch next to me."
"There's no sense in sitting on a fence," said
  the goose. "I don't want to fall. It's much
  better here on the grass!"
"Oh, no, it's better on a perch! Ko-ko-ko!"
  cried the rooster.
"Oh, no, it's better on the grass! Ga-ga-ga!"
  said the goose.
  They argued and argued.
  Ga-ga-ga! Ko-ko-ko! Ga-ga-ga! Ko-ko-ko!
  But they could not come to an agreement.

Then they saw a crow flying in the sky. She flew and she flew, till she settled at the very top of a tall birch tree.

"Tell us, crow, which is
the better place—a perch,
or the grass?" asked the
goose and the rooster.
"Caw-caw-caw! The best
place is a tall, tall tree,
right here where I am,"
said the crow.

The goose and the rooster went down the street
till they saw a pig's snout sticking out of a puddle
near the pigsty.

"Tell us, pig, which is the best place—a perch, or
the grass, or a tall, tall tree?" asked the goose
and the rooster.

"Hroo-hroo-hroo!" grunted the pig. "The best place
is a nice, cool puddle, right here where I am."

The goose and the rooster went out into the field
and saw a little mound of earth moving and rising.
It was the mole digging his burrow, pushing up
the earth.
"Tell us, mole, which is the best place—a perch,
or the grass, or a tall, tall tree, or a nice, cool
puddle?" asked the goose and the rooster.
"The best place is a burrow, right here where I am,"
answered the mole.

The goose and the rooster came to the woods and saw
a squirrel leaping from tree to tree.
"Tell us, squirrel, which is the best place—a perch, or the
grass, or a tall, tall tree, or a puddle, or a burrow?"
asked the goose and the rooster.

The squirrel slipped into
the hollow of a tree and
said, "The best place is
a hollow in a tree, right
here where I am."

The goose and the rooster went on till they came
to a brook and saw a carp in the water. The carp
was not swimming. He stood still among the
reeds, goggling his round eyes and stirring his fins
a little now and then.

"Tell us, carp, which is the best place—a perch,
or the grass, or a tall, tall tree, or a puddle, or
a burrow, or the squirrel's hollow?" asked the
goose and the rooster.

"The best place is the quiet brook, right here
where I am," said the carp.

The goose and the rooster went on and on, till they
came upon a beetle crawling up a tree trunk.
"Tell us, beetle, which is the best place—a perch, or the
grass, or a tall, tall tree, or a puddle, or a burrow,

or the squirrel's hollow, or a quiet brook?" asked the
goose and the rooster.
"The best place is right here where I am," said the beetle,
and he crawled away under the bark.

And now the goose and the rooster were very tired.
They turned around and started out for home.
In the garden near the house, they found Kitty
lying in the hammock.
"Tell us, Kitty, which is the best place—a perch,
or the grass, or a tall, tall tree, or a puddle,
or a burrow, or the squirrel's hollow, or a quiet
brook, or the beetle's home under the bark?"
asked the goose and the rooster.
But Kitty was fast asleep and said nothing.

The rooster flew up to his perch on the fence,
the goose settled down on the fresh green grass,
and they began to wait for Kitty to wake up
and tell them which is the best place of all. They
waited and waited, till they became sleepy too.
They got sleepier and sleepier,
and their eyes began to close.

And there they are now,
still asleep—
the rooster on his perch,
the goose in the grass,
and Kitty in her hammock.

And all the other creatures are sleeping too—
the crow in the tree, the pig in the puddle,
the mole in his burrow, the squirrel in his hollow,
the carp in the brook, and the beetle in his
little nook in the dark, under the bark.